For Mom and Dad,
Elizabeth, Anna, and Krystyna

First published in the United States 1988 by
Dial Books for Young Readers
A Division of NAL Penguin Inc.
2 Park Avenue
New York, New York 10016
Published in Great Britain by Methuen Children's Books
Text copyright © 1988 by Joe Majewski
Pictures copyright © 1988 by Maria Majewska
All rights reserved / Printed in Belgium
First Edition
OBE
2 4 6 8 10 9 7 5 3 1

Library of Congress Cataloging in Publication Data
Majewski, Joe. A friend for Oscar Mouse.
Summary: Oscar, a mouse who lives in the big house,
ventures out into the countryside where his new friend,
Alfie, shows him the ups and downs of living
in the wild with other animals.
[1. Mice — Fiction. 2. Animals — Fiction.]
I. Majewska, Maria, ill. II. Title.
PZ7.M2796Fr 1988   [E]   86-32879
ISBN 0-8037-0348-1

A FRIEND FOR OSCAR MOUSE

by *Joe Majewski* • pictures by *Maria Majewska*

Dial Books for Young Readers • New York

Oscar Mouse lived in an old sugar tin in a little, dark cupboard in a large country house.

Oscar's favorite game was exploring. All day long he would creep around the house, peeping into every nook and cranny, looking for adventure.

But Oscar had to be very careful. The house cat was always ready to pounce on a passing mouse.

One day as he was tiptoeing along a corridor, Oscar noticed a
small hole in the wall. A bright beam of sunlight was shining in.
"I wonder what's on the other side," said Oscar.

He poked his head out. What a dazzling light! He shut his
eyes tight. Then, very slowly, he opened them, one at a time.

"Great cheeses!" he squeaked.

It was a beautiful sunny day. Birds were singing happily in the trees, and a country garden — full of colors and sweet smells — was before him.

Oscar jumped out and landed in a flower bed. To a little mouse it was like a forest.

Butterflies and bees were flitting from flower to flower. Oscar stretched up to sniff each one.

"My, oh my," he kept saying as he scampered about. "So many new things to see." Oscar was so busy looking around, he did not watch where he was going.

Suddenly — bump! He walked into something. He stared wide-eyed at a small furry face.

"Hello," said the furry face. "Who are you?"

"I'm Oscar," he replied. "I come from the big house, but I've never been out here before."

"My name's Alfie, and I'm a field mouse," said the other mouse. "I'll show you around the place."

They went to see the greenhouse . . .

and the bees' house . . .

and the chicken coop.

They climbed in the rock garden . . .

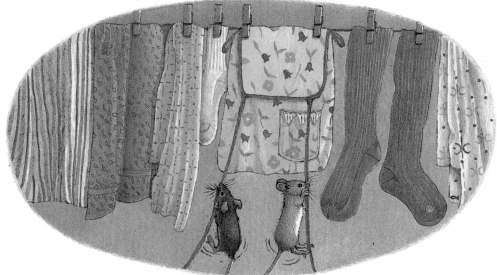

went for a swing . . .

and played hide-and-seek in the garden shed.

But the most exciting place of all was the pond.

"Look at all that water!" Oscar squeaked.

"The water lilies make good stepping-stones," said Alfie.
"I'll race you to the other side."

"Last one across is a fat rat!" yelled Oscar.

They jumped from leaf to leaf . . .

but in the middle of the pond the leaves were wet and slippery.
  Slip! Skid! Splash! Oscar fell in.
  "Help!" he cried. "I can't swim."

Alfie knew what to do. He dangled his tail in the water so that
Oscar could grab hold of it. Alfie pulled and pulled as hard as
he could, and at last out came Oscar, dripping wet and shivering.

Suddenly they heard a loud "Quack!" behind them.

"You've been swimming in *my* part of the pond," said a large duck angrily.

"Oh, I do beg your pardon," said Oscar, and the two mice scurried back to dry land.

"Don't worry," said Alfie. "You'll soon dry out in the sun," and he looked for something to cheer Oscar up.

He soon found the perfect treat.

After eating half a dozen big juicy blackberries, Oscar felt much better. "I'd like to see what's outside the garden gate," he said.

"All right," said Alfie. "Let's go."

An old oak tree stood just outside the gate, and underneath it was a large pile of acorns.

"What's this?" asked Oscar. "Are they nice to eat?"

"I don't think you should touch them," replied Alfie. "That's a very neat pile of acorns. They didn't just fall off the tree."

Oscar was about to pick one up when, quick as a flash,
a squirrel darted up to him.

"Hey! Those are mine!" he shouted.

"Sorry," said Oscar, then turning to Alfie he whispered,
"What a greedy guy. I was only going to try one or two."

Further on Oscar saw something very interesting.

"A fantastic mousehole!" he shouted. "Must be the home of a Very Important Mouse."

"Shhhh, Oscar," whispered Alfie, "and come away from there. We mustn't wake *him* up."

Suddenly out popped a fox's head. He was a bit surprised to see the mice because he never had visitors.

"Hello, little mice. Would you like to come in for a chat?" he asked with a sly grin.

"No, thank you!" shrieked Oscar and Alfie, and they dashed away as fast as they could.

"What a horrible monster!" panted Oscar. "He had even bigger teeth and fiercer eyes than the house cat."

They had hardly got their breath back when the sunshine vanished and the sky turned dark.

"What's happening?" asked Oscar anxiously. Before his friend could answer — plop! A big fat raindrop fell on Oscar's nose and made him jump.

"Whassat!" he squeaked.

The rain came pouring down.

"Oh, no! I'm all wet again," grumbled Oscar, dragging his tail through a puddle.

"It's time we were inside," said Alfie. "My home is not far. Follow me, quick!"

Alfie's mousehole was under a hedge. It was very cozy
with a carpet of moss and feathers. They sat down to a supper of
hazelnuts and mushrooms with one strawberry each for dessert.
  "Yummy!" said Oscar. He soon forgot about the rain and
the horrible fox.

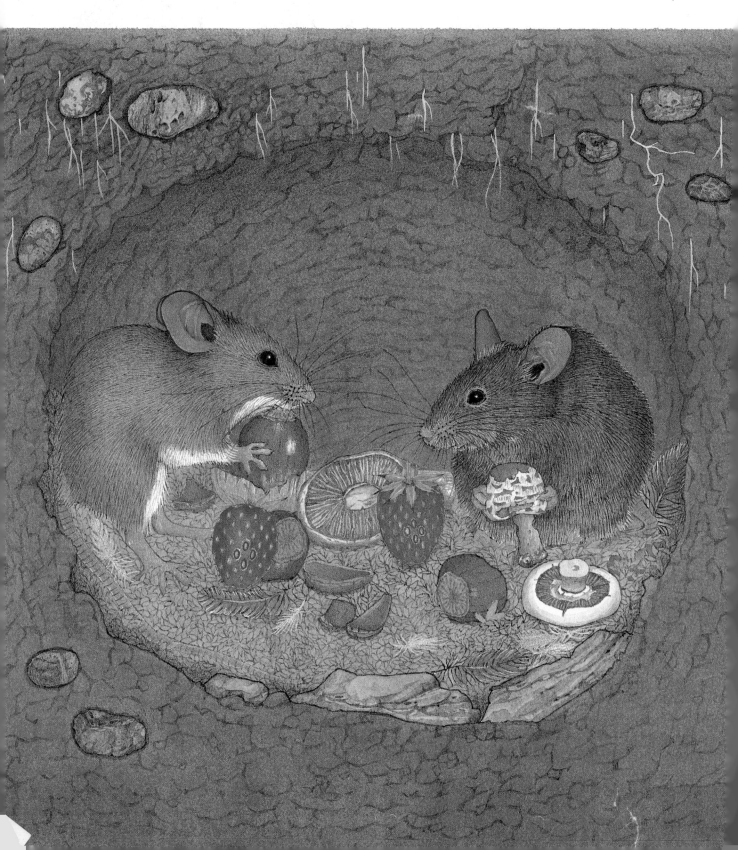

At last it was time for Oscar to go home. Alfie showed him the
way back to the big house, and they said good-bye, promising
each other they would meet again soon.

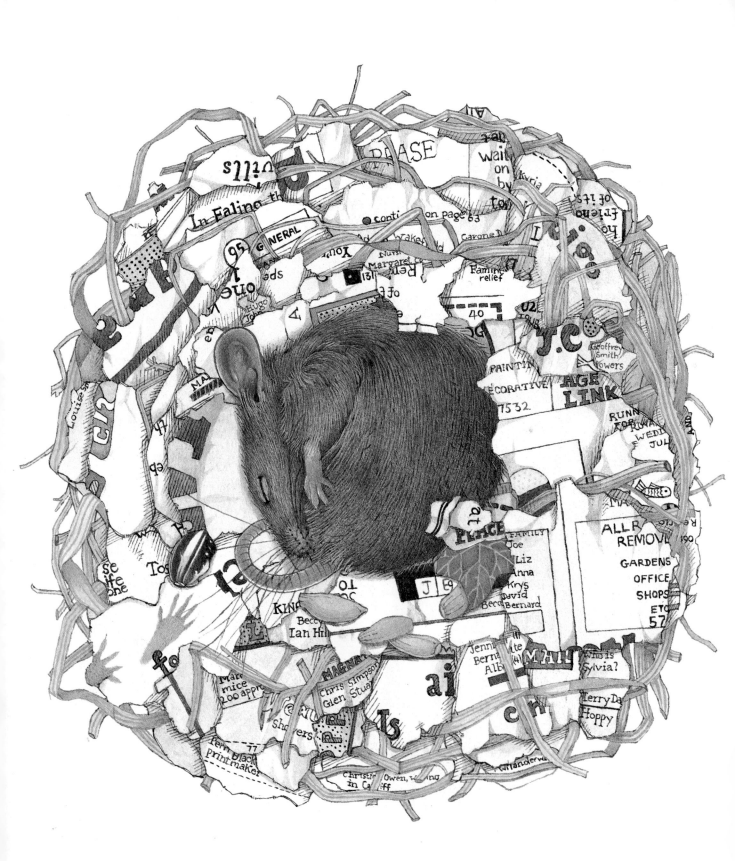

Oscar curled up to sleep in his sugar tin. He was very tired
but happy. He had spent a wonderful day exploring, and best
of all, he had found a friend.